ONE SMART COOKIE

by John Nez

Albert Whitman & Company, Morton Grove, Illinois

*This book is dedicated to secrets that only readers know . . .
and to pets, who already seem to know life's important secrets.*

Library of Congress Cataloging-in-Publication Data
Nez, John A.
One smart Cookie / written and illustrated by John Nez. p. cm.
Summary: When Cookie, a dog who can read and write, goes to school, he not only inspires
the children there, he also helps avert disaster.
ISBN-10: 0-8075-6099-5 (hardcover)
ISBN-13: 978-0-8075-6099-0 (hardcover)
[1. Dogs—Fiction. 2. Reading—Fiction. 3. Writing—Fiction. 4. Schools—Fiction.
5. Fire—Fiction.] I. Title.
PZ7.N4882One 2006 [E]—dc22 2006000004

The design is by Carol Gildar and John Nez.

For information about Albert Whitman & Company,
please visit our web site at www.albertwhitman.com.

Cookie liked to read.
He read the back of the cereal box.
He read the Sunday paper.
He even read junk mail.
The odd thing was that Cookie was a dog.

No one knew how a dog had learned to read.
"I wonder if it could be the glasses," Mom said.
"Or maybe he learned from watching us all read
the newspaper," Dad suggested.

"He wasn't watching me, that's for sure," said Duffy. She never read. All she ever liked to do was draw.

"It couldn't have been from watching me," said Nash. He liked playing *Space Army* all day.

"Perhaps you two should watch Cookie once in a while," said their mom. "You could really learn something."

"How do we know he's even reading?" Nash wondered.

"Maybe he's just looking at the pictures," said Duffy.

"What's the big deal about reading anyhow?" Nash said. "It's not like Cookie can talk."

But it wasn't long before they discovered . . .

Cookie could *write,* too!

"Oh, my goodness!" said Dad. "Next thing you know, he'll be painting pictures and playing the flute."

"Dad, *I'm* the family artist . . . remember?" said Duffy.

Soon Cookie was helping out in the kitchen.
He read recipes for Mom.

"Oh, thank you, Cookie!" she said. "What
would I do without you?"

Cookie read the car repair book to help Dad fix the spark plugs.

"Thanks, Cookie! You're a lifesaver!" said Dad.

At school it was Pets' Day.

The classroom was filled with dogs, cats, hamsters, frogs, and fish. Duffy brought in Cookie.

Duffy stood up when it was her turn.

"This is my dog, Cookie. He's so smart he can read and write real words!" Duffy proudly declared.

The whole class broke out laughing.

"This I gotta see!" Yumi yelled.

"Yeah, show us," said Tommy.

"He's just a dumb dog!" said Cecil.
"He doesn't read . . . he's just like you!"
Everyone laughed. "Dumb dog!
Dumb dog! Can't read!" they all shouted.

"Children! Quiet!" cried Mrs. Woodruff.
"Now where is Cookie, anyway?"
"He's out in the hall," said Bessy.
"And he's doing something really weird!"

"Oh my gosh!" said Mrs. Woodruff. "This dog really *can* read and write!"

"That's what I tried to tell you!" Duffy reminded them.

After that, Cookie was given his own seat in the back of the class.

Smart Cookie!

Good dog, Cookie!

He soon became the class favorite. Some of the kids even called him "Teacher's Pet."

In the lunchroom, Cookie now sat where Duffy used to sit.

"I want to sit by Cookie at lunch!" said Mitsy.

"I want to take Cookie to the library," said Arthur.

Cookie spent lots of time in the library. He read books
about pirates, rocket ships, and dinosaurs. Detective stories
were his favorites.

Cookie made it to the finals of the All-School Spelling Bee.
It was the first time a dog had ever entered the contest.
"Spell 'spaghetti,'" said Mr. Abbott, the judge.

Maggie Bromwell spelled out S-P-A-G-H-E-T-T-I.
She was the school spelling champion.
"Correct!" said Mr. Abbott.

"Now, Cookie, it's your turn," said Mr. Abbott. "Spell 'snorkle.'"
Cookie whined and looked at Duffy.

"Come on Cookie! Don't be nervous!" said Duffy. "'Snorkle,'
Cookie. Come on."

Cookie spelled out S-M-O-K-E.

"Try again, Cookie," Duffy urged. "You can do it!"

This time Cookie spelled out S-M-E-L-L.

"Incorrect!" said Mr. Abbott.

"He's just nervous to be on stage with everyone watching," said Duffy.

Cookie jumped off the stage and ran barking up the aisle. Duffy chased after him.

"Well now, that's against the rules," said Mr. Abbott.
"I'm afraid Cookie loses the match to Maggie Bromwell."

Cookie ran out to the hall and down the stairs to the basement. Duffy ran after him.

"Cookie, where are you going?" she cried. "Why are you running away?"

No one was around in the basement. Something smelled funny. It smelled like . . .

IN AN EMERGENCY

Activate the fire alarm and call 911.

Crawl if there's smoke.

Feel doors for heat before opening.

Never open a hot door with smoke behind it.

Go to the nearest exit.

Leave the building.

Always use an exit stair, not an elevator.

Close doors and windows.

Use a fire extinguisher if the fire is small.

Suddenly Duffy knew why Cookie had written SMOKE SMELL. Because there *was* a smoke smell! This was an emergency!

Duffy looked around and saw a sign that said IN AN EMERGENCY. She read it carefully. Then she heard Cookie barking down the hall.

Cookie was at the door to the furnace room. Black smoke billowed out from under the door, and Cookie barked and barked.

But Duffy had just read the sign. It said, "Never open a hot door with smoke behind it." Duffy felt the door with the back of her hand. It was hot!

"We should leave the door closed and find a fire alarm," Duffy told Cookie. "That's what I read!"

They found the fire alarm, but Duffy didn't know what to do next . . . until she read: "Lift cover up from bottom and pull handle out."

Duffy followed the directions, and soon the fire alarm bells started clanging. It was the most wonderful sound in the world to Duffy.

She had done the right things—all by reading!

The whole school quickly evacuated as three fire trucks pulled up outside.

Soon news reporters arrived, too!

The firefighters quickly put out the fire.

"Well, Miss, I think we can thank you and your dog for saving the school!" the head firefighter told Duffy.

The next morning at the breakfast table, Duffy read aloud the headline from the morning newspaper: "Girl & Dog Save School."

Then Duffy read the whole article to Cookie.

"It says here that you'll be getting a medal, Cookie! Of course I'll have to read a speech for you. I'd better start practicing!"

Nash read the paper, too. "Way cool!" he said. "There's a story on page twelve about a new upgrade to *Space Army*. Awesome!"

After all that excitement, things quieted down to normal around the house. Only now, there seemed to be a lot more reading going on.

In fact, everyone was reading almost as much as Cookie.